Heidi

Johanna Spyri

Condensed and Adapted by
MARY CAPRIO

Illustrated by
JON SAYER

Cover Illustrated by
JESSIE WILLCOX SMITH

Dalmatian Press

The Junior Classics have been
adapted and illustrated with care and thought
to introduce you to a world of famous authors, characters, ideas,
and great stories that have been loved for generations.

Editor — Kathryn Knight
Creative Director — Gina Rhodes-Haynes
And the entire classics project team
of Dalmatian Publishing Group

HEIDI

Copyright © 2011 Dalmatian Press, LLC,
an imprint of Dalmatian Publishing Group.
Franklin, Tennessee 37067 • 1-866-418-2572

ISBN: 1-40377-702-0

Printed in the United States of America

CE13163/0111 CLI

A *note to the reader*—

A classic story rests in your hands. The characters are famous. The tale is timeless.

This Junior Classic edition of *Heidi* has been carefully condensed and adapted from the original version (which you really *must* read when you're ready for every detail). We kept the well-known phrases for you. We kept Johanna Spyri's style. And we kept the important imagery and heart of the tale.

Literature is terrific fun! It encourages you to think. It helps you dream. It is full of heroes and villains, suspense and humor, adventure and wonder, and new ideas. It introduces you to writers who reach out across time to say: "Do you want to hear a story I wrote?"

Curl up and enjoy.

CONTENTS

CHARACTERS

HEIDI — a young orphan girl who comes to live with her Grandfather on Alm Mountain

GRANDFATHER, OR UNCLE — Heidi's grandfather, also called Alm Uncle or Uncle by the villagers

DETIE — Heidi's selfish aunt who brings her to Grandfather

BARBEL — a friend of Detie's

PETER — the boy who tends the goats on Alm Mountain

GRANDMOTHER — Peter's grandmother

BRIGITTA — Peter's mother

CHARACTERS

CLARA SESEMANN — a girl in Frankfurt, Germany, who must use a wheelchair, and who receives Heidi as her new companion

MR. SESEMANN — Clara's father

MISS ROTTENMEIER — the Sesemann family's housekeeper

SEBASTIAN — the thoughtful butler at the Sesemann house

TINETTE — the maid at the Sesemann house

GRANDMAMMA (MRS. SESEMANN) — Clara's grandmother

THE DOCTOR — an old friend of the Sesemann family, a new friend for Heidi and her grandfather

Heidi

CHAPTER ONE

Up the Mountain

At the foot of the beautiful Swiss mountains lies the small village of Mayenfeld. From this village there leads a narrow mountain footpath that travels through green meadows, into the little town of Dörfli, and then on up to the very top of the Alm Mountain.

On a sunny morning in June, a tall young woman and a little girl, who looked about five years old, were climbing the path. The woman's name was Detie and the little girl was her niece, Heidi. Even though it was a hot day, the child was wearing two dresses and a shawl. She was so hot that her face was bright red.

About halfway up the mountain, they came to the town of Dörfli. Detie used to live there and many of the people said hello to her. A young woman named Barbel came out to walk with them.

"Is this your sister's little girl?" asked Barbel.

"Yes," answered Detie. "I am taking her to stay with Uncle."

"That grumpy old man? He'll never do it!" Barbel exclaimed.

"He has to," said Detie. "He is her grandfather. I have a new job working as a maid for a rich family in Frankfurt, Germany. I have taken care of Heidi since my sister died, but now it is his turn."

"I can't believe you would leave a little girl with him," Barbel told her. "He lives all alone up there and won't talk to anyone when he comes into town. Why does he act so mean?"

"I will tell you, but you can't tell anyone else." Detie looked around to make sure that Heidi couldn't hear them, but the child was gone.

"I see her!" Barbel cried. "She is over there with Peter the goat boy."

Every day Peter brought the goats up from Dörfli to eat the plants that grew on the

mountain. In the afternoon, he brought them back to Dörfli and their owners came to get them. Heidi was happily running in and out of his flock.

After finding Heidi, Detie went on with her story. "When Uncle was a young man, he wasted all of his father's money. His parents died soon after and Uncle went away to be a soldier. Many years later he came back with a little boy. It was his son, Tobias. His wife had died soon after they married. He asked his relatives to take Tobias in, but none of them wanted to help. That's when Uncle moved to Dörfli. The people here liked Tobias. He worked as a carpenter when he was grown and married my sister, Adelaide. Four years ago, Tobias died in an accident. Adelaide was sick and died soon after, leaving Heidi with me."

"Why does everyone call the old man Uncle?" Barbel asked.

Detie said, "My family calls him Uncle because my great-grandmother was his grand-mother's sister. Since so many people in Dörfli are related to us, almost everyone started calling him Uncle."

"Why did he leave Dörfli to live alone on the mountain?" Barbel wanted to know.

"After Tobias and Adelaide died, some people said that their deaths were God's way of punishing Uncle. This made him so angry that he did not want to live among people anymore," Detie answered.

The two women came to a small, broken-down hut. This was where Peter lived. His grandmother did spinning and Barbel had work for her to do. Barbel said good-bye to Detie and went inside.

Detie stood outside the hut, looking all around. The children and the goats were nowhere to be seen.

Peter and Heidi were taking a different path. Heidi was getting very hot from all the clothes she was wearing. Looking at Peter in his short pants and bare feet, she decided to take off her shoes and stockings. Next came the hot red shawl and both dresses. She stood up in her petticoat and laughed. Heidi left her extra clothes in a pile on the ground and kept climbing with the goats. She asked Peter lots of questions about what the goats ate and where they were going. She wanted to know everything!

When they came to Peter's hut, Detie was waiting. She was very angry when she saw Heidi. "Where have you left your clothes, you thoughtless child?"

The little girl pointed down the mountain to where her little pile of clothes lay. She did not look sorry at all.

"Well, who is going all the way back down to get them?" Detie demanded. "Peter, fetch them as fast as you can and I will give you this." She held out a bright new coin.

Peter ran down the mountainside, taking the shortest way possible. He grabbed the clothes and raced back. Detie gave him the money. He put the coin in his pocket and grinned. He did not have money of his own very often.

The three of them began walking again. After almost an hour, they came to a hut with three giant fir trees behind it. They could see the whole valley from up there.

An old man was sitting on a bench out front. Heidi knew this must be her grandfather. She went over to him and said, "Hello, Grandfather."

"Who are you?" he asked. He stared at her, and

Heidi stared right back. She had never seen anyone with such a long, gray beard and thick eyebrows.

"Hello, Uncle," said Detie. "This is your son's child, Heidi. I have brought her here to stay with you."

"Why would I want her here?" the old man asked roughly. "You there," he called to Peter. "Take those goats up the mountain now!"

Peter hurried away.

"She is here to stay," Detie told Uncle. "I have taken care of her for four years. Now it is up to you."

She said a quick good-bye to Heidi and then hurried down the path toward Dörfli.

CHAPTER TWO

At Home with Grandfather

After Detie left, Heidi took a look around. Next to the hut, she found the shed where the goats lived. Then she went to see the giant fir trees that stood behind the hut. The wind was strong and made a great rushing noise through their branches.

She went back to where her grandfather was sitting. "I want to see what your house is like," she told him.

"Let's go," he said as he stood up. "Bring your clothes."

"I don't need them," Heidi answered. "I'm going to run around like Peter, with no shoes on."

"Well, you can if you like," her grandfather said, "but bring them in so we can put them away."

The old man opened the door and Heidi went in. The hut was one big room. There was a table and chair near the fireplace, and her grandfather's bed was in the corner. Grandfather kept his clothes, dishes and food in a large cupboard against one wall. Heidi put her clothes in there, way in the back so they would be hard to find.

"Where will I sleep, Grandfather?" she asked.

"Where would you like to sleep?"

In the corner near her grandfather's bed, she found a short ladder leading up to the hayloft. There was a large pile of fresh hay up there and a round window to look out of.

"I will sleep here, Grandfather," she called down to him. "It's so nice up here!"

Heidi pushed all the hay into a big pile so she could use it for a bed. "Do you have a sheet for me?" she asked.

Her grandfather looked around in the cupboard and found a long piece of fabric. He carried it up to the loft.

"I need one more thing, Grandfather," said Heidi. "A bedspread. When you get into bed, you

crawl in between the sheet and the bedspread."

He went down the ladder and came back with a heavy sack. It was just the right size for a bedspread.

"Perfect!" Heidi said. "I wish I could go to sleep right now!"

"I think we should have something to eat first," said Grandfather.

"I think so, too!" Heidi said quickly. After a long day of walking in the sun, she was very hungry.

The old man followed Heidi down the ladder. He went to the fire and toasted a large piece of cheese on a long iron fork until the cheese was golden brown on both sides.

While he was doing that, Heidi set the table. She brought the plates and knives from the cupboard, along with a loaf of bread she found there.

"Good, but what will you do for a seat?" her grandfather asked. There was only one chair. Heidi ran to get the little stool that was sitting by the fire. She sat down on it, only to find it was too short for her to reach the table.

Grandfather had an idea. He pushed his chair over to her so she could use it as a table. He gave her a big slice of bread, a piece of cheese, and a

bowl of milk. Then he sat down on the corner of the table and ate his own supper.

Heidi took the bowl with both hands and drank until the milk was gone. That long walk had made her quite thirsty.

"This is the best milk I have ever had!" Heidi exclaimed.

"Then have some more." He filled her bowl again. Heidi happily ate her bread and cheese, stopping sometimes for a drink of milk.

When they were done, Grandfather swept out the goats' shed and put in fresh straw for them to sleep on. Next, he cut three long sticks and a small, round board. He made three holes in the board and pounded the sticks into them.

"What do you think it is?" Grandfather asked Heidi.

"It's a stool for me! I know it is, because it's so tall!" Heidi answered.

Later they heard a loud whistle. It was Peter and the goats. One white goat and one brown goat ran to Grandfather. He had salt in his hands for them and they licked it up. Peter waved and went down with the rest of the flock.

Heidi petted the pretty goats. "Are they ours?

What are their names?"

"Yes. The white one is Little Swan and the brown one is Little Bear," Grandfather answered.

That night, the wind was stormy and loud. Grandfather went up to see if Heidi was scared by the noise. She was sound asleep on her bed of hay. Even in her sleep, she was smiling.

CHAPTER THREE

Out with the Goats

Heidi woke up the next morning when she heard Peter's whistle. She dressed quickly and ran outside. Grandfather was bringing out Little Swan and Little Bear. "Do you want to go with Peter today?" he asked Heidi. She jumped for joy.

"First you have to wash your face and hands. We don't want the sun to laugh at you because you're dirty," said her grandfather. He had a tub of water ready and Heidi scrubbed until she was shiny.

Grandfather took Peter into the hut to give him bread and cheese for Heidi's lunch. Peter opened his eyes wide when he saw how much food there was. It was much more than he had for himself.

"Here is a little bowl. At lunchtime, fill it twice with milk from the white goat," Grandfather told him. "Be careful that Heidi does not fall over the rocks, do you hear?"

The sun was shining and Heidi ran about, filling her apron with colorful flowers. The goats wanted to run around with her. It was hard for Peter to keep them all together.

"Come here," called Peter to Heidi. "You have enough flowers! If you pick them all today, there won't be any left for tomorrow."

They came to the spot where the goats liked to eat. Peter found a spot to put his lunch bag where it wouldn't blow away. Then he lay down and went to sleep.

Heidi put her flowers next to Peter's bag and looked around. The little town of Dörfli was far below. In front of her, she could see a big field of snow on the side of the mountain. To her left were the sharp rocks that Grandfather had warned Peter about.

She heard a loud cry and saw a large bird flying in circles above them.

"Peter, wake up!" she called. "Look how big that bird is!"

Peter sat up. They watched the bird until it went behind the mountaintops.

"Where did it go?" asked Heidi.

"Home to its nest," said Peter.

"Let's climb up there and find it," Heidi suggested.

"Oh, no! Even the goats can't climb that high! Uncle would be mad at me if I let you climb the rocks."

Instead, Heidi played with the goats. Some of them were eating. Others were playing or pushing each other with their horns. She wanted to get to know them all.

At noon, Peter got out the lunch bag. He placed the pieces of bread and cheese on a cloth on the ground. The bigger ones were Heidi's and the smaller ones were his. Then he took the bowl and put some milk in it from the white goat.

"Here is your milk," Peter told Heidi. "The big pieces of bread and cheese are yours, too. Drink up the milk and I will get you some more."

Heidi broke off some bread and gave the rest to Peter. "You can have this," she told him. "I can't eat it all."

Peter was not used to people sharing their food with him. When he saw she really meant it, he thanked her.

As they ate, Peter told Heidi the names of all the goats. Turk was the one with the big horns. He liked to push around the smaller goats. Then there was little Greenfinch. She wasn't afraid of anything! Snowflake was the smallest. She said *"baa-aa"* so sadly that Heidi wanted to know what was wrong with her.

Peter explained. "Snowflake cries because her mother isn't here. She was sold the day before yesterday."

"Poor Snowflake!" cried Heidi. She hugged the little animal. "Don't cry. I will come every day to see you. You are not alone anymore."

All of a sudden, Peter jumped up and ran after one of the goats. Heidi followed him to see what was wrong. Peter had seen Greenfinch heading toward the sharp rocks. He wanted to catch her before she fell over the edge. Peter dropped down on his stomach and grabbed her back legs. Greenfinch was mad at being stopped and she fought to get away. Peter called for Heidi to help him.

Heidi quickly picked some leaves and held them out to Greenfinch. "Come with me, Greenfinch!"

The animal turned away from the rocks. As she ate the leaves, Peter stood up and grabbed Greenfinch's collar. He walked her back to the other goats. Peter was so mad that he wanted to hit the goat with his stick.

Heidi cried out, "No, Peter. You must not punish her. See how scared she is!"

Peter slowly let the stick drop. "Alright," said Peter, "I don't care," which meant that he would do as she asked.

It was afternoon now and the sun was going behind the high mountains. The sun touched the grass and flowers with a beautiful golden light. The rocks on the mountainside started to glow and the snowfield turned pink.

"Look, Peter! The rocks and the sky are burning," Heidi shouted.

"It is not really burning," Peter told her. He was not excited at all.

"Oh, no, now all the color has gone away! The mountains are turning dark. It's all gone, Peter," said Heidi, in a sad voice.

"It will come again tomorrow," said Peter. "Now it's time to go home." He whistled for the goats and they started down the mountain.

When they got to the hut, Heidi said good night to Peter and hugged little Snowflake.

"Oh, Grandfather!" Heidi cried. "It was so beautiful! I saw the fire on the mountain, the big bird, and everything. Look what I brought you!" She opened her apron, but the flowers were all dry and brown.

"What is wrong with them, Grandfather?" Heidi asked with surprise.

"They like to be outside in the sun, and not shut up in an apron," said her grandfather.

"Then I won't pick any more," Heidi decided.

She told him how everything turned bright and rosy at the end of the day. Grandfather said that it was the sun that did that. "When the sun says good night, he shows the mountains his most beautiful colors. That way they won't forget him during the night."

Heidi Goes Visiting

Heidi went with Peter and the goats every day that summer. When fall came, the winds blew harder and some days her grandfather kept her home.

Peter hated those days. He was lonely without Heidi and missed the good food she brought with her, too.

Since it was getting colder, Heidi went to the cupboard and got out her shoes, stockings, and dresses. When the snow started to fall, Peter no longer came in the mornings.

One night there was a heavy fall of snow. The next morning the whole mountain was covered

with it. When the snow stopped, Grandfather cleared it away from the door and windows.

They soon had a visitor. It was Peter, covered in snow from head to toe. He came in and stood by the fire. As the snow started to melt from his clothes, he looked like a waterfall!

"How are you, Peter?" asked Grandfather. "Now that winter is here, you can go to school again."

Heidi wanted to know all about school. She asked Peter so many questions that his clothes were dry by the time she finished.

Before Peter left, he told Heidi, "My grandmother would like you to come and see her."

Heidi wanted to go the next morning, but the snow was too deep. A few days later, her grandfather brought down the sack from Heidi's bed. "It's time to go visiting," he said.

He pulled a large sled out from the shed. He sat on the seat and Heidi sat on his lap. Grandfather wrapped her in the sack to keep warm. He pushed off with his feet and the sled raced down the mountain. Heidi felt as if they were flying like a bird!

At Peter's hut, Grandfather helped Heidi off.

"When it gets dark, it's time to come home," he told her, then he pulled the sled back up the mountain.

Heidi opened the door. Inside, the hut was the same size as her grandfather's, but most of the things in it were falling apart. Heidi saw a woman sewing near the door and she thought this must be Peter's mother. There was an old woman in the corner, working on a spinning wheel. Heidi went to her and said, "Good day, Grandmother. Here I am."

The woman looked up and reached out for Heidi's hand. "Are you Heidi?"

"Yes," the little girl answered. "I just came down in the sled with Grandfather."

"What does she look like, Brigitta?" the old woman asked.

Peter's mother looked at the little girl closely. "She is small like Adelaide, but her hair is curly like her father's and grandfather's."

While the women talked, Heidi was looking at everything in the room. All of a sudden she noticed a loud noise.

"Grandmother, one of your shutters is banging against the window. Do you see it?"

"Dear child," said Grandmother. "I cannot see it, but I hear it. When the wind blows, everything rattles and the cold creeps in all the cracks. We don't have anyone to fix it since Peter doesn't know how."

"Why can't you see the shutter, Grandmother? Look, there it goes again!" Heidi pointed.

Grandmother explained to Heidi that she was blind. When Heidi understood that the woman could not see anything, she began to cry.

"Come, let me tell you something," Grandmother said. "I am so glad to have you here to talk to. Tell me how you like living up there with your grandfather."

Heidi stopped crying. She told Grandmother how she liked to go out with the goats and how much fun it was to watch Grandfather make things with his tools.

Peter came home while they were talking.

"Back from school already, Peter?" his grandmother asked. "This afternoon went by so fast! How are you doing with your reading?"

"Just the same," said the boy.

"You are almost twelve. You should be able to read by now," said the old woman sadly.

She turned to Heidi. "Up there on that shelf is a beautiful old prayer book. I hoped that Peter would read it to me, but he says it is too hard."

"I must get a light," Brigitta said then, putting down her sewing.

"If it's getting dark, it's time for me to go," Heidi told them. She said good-bye and went outside. There her grandfather was waiting to walk her back.

When they got home, Heidi told him, "Grandfather, tomorrow we must take your tools down to Grandmother's house. We need to fix the shutter and stop the house from rattling."

"We do? Who told you that?" he asked.

"Nobody told me. I just know it," said Heidi. "Everything is falling apart, but I know that you can fix it."

She hugged her grandfather and looked up at him hopefully. He thought for a minute and then said, "Yes, Heidi. Tomorrow we will go fix things."

He kept his promise. The next day when they went to Grandmother's, Heidi went inside and Grandfather went around behind the house.

Just as Heidi said "Hello," there was a loud banging outside. Grandmother cried, "The house is falling down!"

Heidi patted her arm and said, "No, it is Grandfather with his hammer. He will fix everything for you."

CHAPTER FIVE

Two Visits and What Came of Them

That winter passed quickly and so did the bright summer that followed. Now another winter was ending. Heidi was eight years old, but had never gone to school. Her grandfather taught her many useful things, but not how to read and write.

The teacher in Dörfli sent letters to Grandfather, asking him to send her to school. Grandfather always said no.

One sunny March morning, Heidi was playing outside. She had just jumped over the water tub for at least the tenth time. She looked up to see an old gentleman dressed in black. She was so surprised she almost fell into the water!

The gentleman smiled. "Don't be afraid. I'm here to see your grandfather."

Heidi took him inside. Her grandfather was at the table, making wooden spoons.

The man said, "Good morning, Uncle."

Grandfather looked up in surprise to see it was the pastor from the Dörfli church.

"Heidi, take some salt out to the goats," said her grandfather. "Stay with them until I come."

Heidi skipped out of the room.

"She should have been in school a year ago," said the pastor. "Why won't you send her?"

"Heidi is safe and happy here, growing up with the goats and the birds. I do not want her to learn evil things down in the village," said Grandfather.

"A child is not a goat or a bird, she is a person! She may not learn evil up here, but she does not learn good things either. I have come now so that you can get ready to send her to school this fall," the pastor told him.

"Do you really want me to send a little girl down the mountain in winter weather?" cried Grandfather angrily. "And have her come back at night? Do you want her to get sick or hurt? I don't. I will not send her!"

"You're right," said the pastor. "It would be wrong to send her to school from here in the winter. You need to come live in Dörfli again."

"The people in the village hate me," Grandfather said. "It is better that we live away from them."

The pastor turned away sadly and went back down the mountain.

This visit left Grandfather in a bad mood. When Heidi wanted to go see Peter's grandmother that afternoon, he said, "Not today."

The next morning they had another visitor. It was Detie wearing a hat with a feather and a long dress. Grandfather was not pleased to see her. She said that she had found a better place for Heidi to live. A rich family in Frankfurt was looking for a girl to live with them and be a friend to their sick daughter.

The grandfather glared at her. "I won't have anything to do with this!"

"The child is eight years old!" Detie cried. "You don't send her to church or to school. She will be better off in Frankfurt. Everyone in Dörfli would agree with me!"

"Be silent," shouted Uncle. "Go! Never let me see you or your fancy feathered hat again!" He marched out of the hut.

"You made Grandfather angry," said Heidi. She did not look very friendly.

"He will get over it. You will love it in Frankfurt." Detie went to the cupboard and rolled Heidi's things up in a bundle.

"I won't go," Heidi told her.

"Don't be stupid!" Detie replied. "You heard him, he wants us to leave. If you don't like it in Frankfurt, you can come back here."

"Can I go to Frankfurt right now and come home tonight?" asked Heidi.

"Today we will go as far as Mayenfeld. Tomorrow we will take the train to Frankfurt. The train will bring you back when you're ready," Detie said.

She put the bundle under her arm and grabbed Heidi's hand. Heidi wanted to stop and say good-bye to Peter's grandmother, but Detie wouldn't let her. She didn't want Heidi to change her mind about going. Detie promised that they would find a nice gift for Grandmother in Frankfurt. Heidi stopped trying to pull away

from Detie when she heard this.

"What could I bring back to her?" Heidi asked.

"How about a soft white roll of bread?" answered Detie. "Now that she is old, the black bread must be hard for her to eat."

"She always gives the black bread to Peter," agreed Heidi. "Let's hurry so we can bring the white rolls back tonight."

From that day on, Uncle looked meaner than ever. He carried his big stick and everyone stayed out of his way. Peter's grandmother was the only one who would say nothing bad about him. She told everyone how good Uncle had been to her family, and how much he loved Heidi.

CHAPTER SIX

A New Chapter About New Things

In Frankfurt, Clara Sesemann was waiting for her new friend to come. Clara was often sick and used a wheelchair since she was too weak to walk. Today she was watching the clock. How slowly it moved!

The housekeeper, Miss Rottenmeier, was waiting with her. Clara's mother had died many years before and her father was often away on business. Miss Rottenmeier took care of Clara and the rest of the household.

At last, the maid, Tinette, came in to say that Detie and her niece had arrived. When Detie and Heidi came into the study, Miss Rottenmeier

came over for a closer look at Heidi. She did not
seem happy with what she saw.

"What's your name, child?" asked Miss
Rottenmeier.

"Heidi," the girl answered.

"What kind of name is that?" the lady said,
shaking her head.

"I'm sorry, Miss," Detie said. "She was
named Adelaide, after her mother. This is her
first time in a gentleman's house. She does not
yet know good manners."

"I told you I wanted a child the same age as
Clara. That way they can take lessons together.
Miss Clara is now twelve. How old is this child?"
Miss Rottenmeier demanded.

"I think she is about ten," said Detie.

"Grandfather said I was eight," put in Heidi.
Detie gave her a poke.

"Only eight!" cried Miss Rottenmeier. "What
books have you read?"

"I don't know how to read," Heidi told her.

"This is not what you promised," the
housekeeper told Detie. "How could you bring
me a child like this?"

"You said you wanted a sweet and gentle

child. That's what she is," Detie told her. "Now I must go back to work." She hurried out.

Miss Rottenmeier followed Detie. She had many more questions about this child.

Clara called Heidi over to her. "Should I call you Heidi or Adelaide?"

"I am always called Heidi," said the child.

"Are you glad to be here, Heidi?"

"No, but I will go home tomorrow. I'm going to take some soft white rolls to Grandmother," explained Heidi.

"You are a funny child!" said Clara. "You're going to stay here with me. You can share my lessons and learn to read. It will be fun."

Heidi shook her head. She did not think she could learn to read.

"Oh, you must learn to read!" Clara told her. "My tutor is very nice. He will teach you your ABC's."

Miss Rottenmeier now came back into the room. She was upset because Detie had left without talking to her. She did not think Heidi would be a good companion for Clara, but now that Detie was gone, she did not know what to do with the child. She was in a very sour mood. She called Tinette and ordered her to get a room

ready for the little girl.

At suppertime, Sebastian, the butler, pushed Clara's wheelchair to the table. Miss Rottenmeier sat next to her and Heidi was across from them. There was a white roll sitting next to Heidi's plate. She asked Sebastian, "Can I have it?"

Sebastian nodded. She put it in her pocket. He tried not to laugh.

Next Sebastian held out a dish of food to her. Heidi didn't understand that she was supposed to take some. "Should I eat some of that?" she asked him.

Sebastian nodded again.

"Give me some then," she told him. Sebastian tried even harder not to laugh! The dish wobbled.

"Put that down and come back later," Miss Rottenmeier scolded him. "Adelaide, do not speak to the servants like they are friends. Talk to them only when you need something. You will call me Miss Rottenmeier. Clara will tell you what she wants you to call her."

"Clara, of course," the young lady said.

Miss Rottenmeier then gave Heidi a long list of rules to learn. There were rules for getting up, going to bed, and everything in between! When the list was done, Miss Rottenmeier asked, "Do you understand, Adelaide?"

"Heidi has been asleep for a long time!" said Clara with a smile.

CHAPTER SEVEN

Miss Rottenmeier Has a Bad Day

When Heidi woke up, she found herself in a big bed with soft pillows. She dressed herself and looked out the window. She could not see the sky or trees, just streets and buildings.

After breakfast, the girls went into the study to wait for Clara's tutor. Clara asked Heidi lots of questions and Heidi had fun telling Clara about Peter and his goats.

Soon the tutor arrived and the girls began their lessons.

All of a sudden, Miss Rottenmeier heard a loud crash. She rushed into the study and found a huge mess. Books, paper, and the inkstand were on the floor. The tablecloth was on top and ink was running across the floor. Heidi was gone.

"What happened?" cried Miss Rottenmeier. "It was that awful child, wasn't it?"

Clara smiled. "Yes, but it was an accident. Carriages were passing by. Heidi heard them and jumped up so fast that she pulled the tablecloth with her."

Miss Rottenmeier found Heidi standing in the open door, looking out at the street.

"Why did you run out like that?" the housekeeper asked.

"I heard the sound of the fir trees, but I can't find them. I can't even hear them now!" answered Heidi. When she had heard the carriages, it sounded to her like the wind in the fir trees back home.

Back in the study, Heidi was surprised to see the big mess. Miss Rottenmeier said, "I know it was an accident, but do not let it happen again! During lessons, you must sit or else I will tie you in your chair."

After the tutor left, Sebastian and Tinette came in to clean up.

Now it was time for Clara to rest. Miss

Rottenmeier told Heidi that she could play quietly by herself. The little girl knew just what she wanted to do. She went looking for Sebastian.

When she found him, she asked him to help her pull back the heavy drapes. He did, but Heidi was too short to see out of the window. He brought her a stool to stand on. She was sad when all she saw were the stony streets.

"Where can I go to see the countryside?" she asked him.

"You would have to climb up a tall tower," he told her, "like that church tower over there with the gold ball at the top."

Heidi went outside. At the corner, she met a boy with a hand-organ on his back. "Can you show me how to get to the church with the tower?" Heidi asked him.

"What will you give me?" said the boy. Heidi looked in her pockets. All she had was a pretty card with roses painted on it. Clara had just given it to her as a present.

She showed the card to the boy. He shook his head no.

"What would you like then?" asked Heidi.

"Money."

"I don't have any, but Clara would give you some. How much do you want?"

"Two pennies."

"Come on then."

They walked down the street. Heidi asked him what he had on his back. He said that it was a hand-organ. It played music when he turned the handle. At last they came to the church.

Heidi saw a bell in the wall and pulled on the bell cord as hard as she could. "If I go up, you have to wait for me. I don't know how to get home by myself."

"Yes, but you'll have to give me another two pennies."

An old man opened the door. He was angry to see them. "Why did you call me? This bell is only for people who want to go up in the tower."

"But I do want to go up there," said Heidi.

"Go home. Don't try this trick again," said the man. He tried to close the door, but Heidi grabbed his coat.

"Please," she begged.

"Well, if you want to that much, I will take you."

The boy sat down to wait. Heidi followed the old man up many steps to get to the top of the tower. At the end, he lifted her up so she could look out the window. All she could see were roofs and chimneys.

"That is not what I thought I would see," she said sadly.

On the way downstairs, Heidi saw a gray cat in a large basket. There were seven or eight tiny kittens climbing around her.

"Oh, how sweet they are!" Heidi laughed as she watched them.

"Would you like one?" the man asked her.

"To keep?" asked Heidi.

"Yes, take all of them if you have room for them," said the old man. "I would be glad to find them a home."

"But how can I take them with me?" asked Heidi.

"I will bring them. Just tell me where the house is," said the old man.

"It is the Sesemann house. The door knocker looks like a dog's head," Heidi explained.

"I know the house," he replied.

Downstairs, the boy was still waiting. Heidi and the boy walked back to the Sesemann house and Heidi rang the bell. Sebastian opened it. When he saw it was Heidi, he quickly brought her inside and closed the door. He had not seen the little organ boy, and the boy was left standing on the steps without his four pennies!

CHAPTER EIGHT

Heidi Causes Trouble

After Clara and Heidi started their lessons the next morning, the doorbell rang. Sebastian answered it, and there stood the ragged little boy with the hand-organ on his back.

"I want to see Clara," the boy told him.

"She is 'Miss Clara' to you, little rascal. What do you want?" asked Sebastian.

"She owes me two pennies for showing how to get to the church and two pennies for showing the way back," the boy explained.

"You are lying! She can't even walk," Sebastian said.

"I saw her in the street," the boy insisted.

"She has short, curly black hair and black eyes."

Aha, thought Sebastian. He laughed and invited the boy inside. "Wait here until I call you. Start playing your hand-organ as soon as you go in the door."

Sebastian went in the study and announced, "There is a boy outside who wants to see Miss Clara."

The boy walked in, playing his organ loudly. Miss Rottenmeier heard the noise and came running.

"Stop at once!" she ordered. She was going to grab the boy, but then she saw something crawling toward her shoe. It was a turtle!

"Get rid of them both!" Miss Rottenmeier shouted.

Sebastian grabbed the boy. The boy picked up his turtle. When they got outside, Sebastian put money in the boy's hand.

"Here are four pennies from Miss Clara. And here are another four pennies for the music. You did great!"

Soon Sebastian knocked on the study door again. This time he brought in a large covered basket. He said that someone had left it for Miss Clara.

"For me?" said Clara. She couldn't wait to open it!

"Finish your work first," Miss Rottenmeier said. Suddenly the cover of the basket came off and kittens came jumping out! They hopped over the tutor's boots, clawed at Miss Rottenmeier's dress, and climbed onto Clara's couch.

The girls laughed and clapped their hands.

Miss Rottenmeier didn't want the kittens to jump on her. She was afraid to get up, so she shouted, "Tinette! Sebastian!"

They came in and put the kittens back in the basket. Sebastian took them upstairs to live where Miss Rottenmeier would not find them.

When Miss Rottenmeier stopped being scared, she was mad. She figured out that the turtle, the boy, and the kittens had all come to the house because of Heidi. She wanted to punish Heidi by sending her down to the dark cellar.

"Oh, no!" Clara said. "Wait until Papa comes home. He will decide what to do about Heidi."

Heidi kept saving her rolls for Grandmother. Each day while Clara rested, Heidi sat alone in her room and thought about how much she missed everyone back home. One day she decided that it was time to leave. Detie had told

her that she could go home when she wanted to, so that's what she would do. Heidi wrapped the rolls in her red shawl and put on her old straw hat. Before Heidi could get outside, she ran into Miss Rottenmeier.

"Where do you think you are going?" Miss Rottenmeier demanded.

Scared, Heidi answered, "I am going home."

"Going home!" said Miss Rottenmeier. "What would Mr. Sesemann think if he knew you wanted to run away?"

Heidi's feelings came pouring out. "I just want to go home! Snowflake will be crying again and Grandmother is waiting for me. I miss my grandfather and I want to see how the sun says good night to the mountains!"

"I don't understand a word of this," cried Miss Rottenmeier. She called for Sebastian to take Heidi up to her room.

Heidi slowly walked back to her room. That night at supper, she sat very still. She didn't talk or eat, but she did put her roll in her pocket.

The next day, Miss Rottenmeier found the rolls Heidi had been hiding in her closet.

"Tinette, get rid of these old rolls," Miss Rottenmeier ordered. "Throw away that ugly straw hat, too."

"No!" screamed Heidi. "That's my hat! The rolls are for Grandmother." She tried to stop Tinette, but Miss Rottenmeier would not let her. The little girl burst into tears.

Heidi's eyes were still red that night at supper. She sat quietly, even though Sebastian was acting funny. When Miss Rottenmeier wasn't looking, he would point to his head and then point to Heidi's.

When Heidi went to bed that night, she found her old hat under her bedspread. Sebastian had saved it for her. That was what he had tried to tell her with those funny signs at supper.

CHAPTER NINE

Mr. Sesemann and Another Grandmother

Mr. Sesemann came home a few days later and rushed in to see his daughter. Heidi was sitting beside her just like always. He hugged Clara, then shook hands with Heidi. "So this is your little friend! Do you get along well?"

The girls told him that they did.

"I'm glad to hear it," said Clara's father. "Please excuse me while I get some dinner. I haven't eaten all day."

Miss Rottenmeier was waiting for him in the dining room. She looked unhappy. "What is the matter?" he asked. "Clara looks happy."

"Clara is fine. It's Heidi," Miss Rottenmeier told him. "You would not believe the people and animals she has brought here! It is bad for Clara to have her here."

Mr. Sesemann ate and went back in the study. He wanted to talk to Clara alone, so he asked Heidi to get him a glass of water.

"Now, Clara," he said when Heidi was gone, "what kind of animals has your little friend brought into the house? Why does Miss Rottenmeier think there is something wrong with her?"

Clara told him about the turtle and the kittens. Mr. Sesemann laughed. Clara also explained how upset Heidi was the day she tried to leave. Her father asked, "Do you want her to stay or should I send her back home?"

"Please let her stay!" Clara answered. "Everything is so much nicer since Heidi came."

"Then that's what we'll do," Mr. Sesemann decided. He turned to Miss Rottenmeier. "My mother will soon be coming for a long visit and *she* will be good to the child."

"Yes, of course," said the housekeeper, without a smile.

Mr. Sesemann was only home for a few days before leaving again. Clara was sad that he had to leave so soon, but happy that her grandmother would be here any day. She talked about her so much that Heidi, too, started to call her "Grandmamma." This did not please Miss Rottenmeier. She told Heidi that when she arrived Heidi was to call her Madam or Mrs. Sesemann.

This confused Heidi. When the little girl finally met Clara's grandmother, she said, "Good evening, Mrs. Madam."

"Is that what they call people on your mountain?" asked Mrs. Sesemann, laughing. "Just call me Grandmamma. Children always do. What is your name?"

"I am Heidi, but I am supposed to be called Adelaide," Heidi told her.

"If Heidi is your name, then I will call you Heidi."

The next day when Clara rested, Grandmamma asked Miss Rottenmeier to send Heidi to her. "I have some pretty books with me. I would like to give them to her."

"The poor girl hasn't even learned her ABC's yet!" Miss Rottenmeier replied.

"That's strange," Mrs. Sesemann said.

"She looks like a smart little girl. Well, at least she can look at the pictures."

When Heidi came in, she was delighted to see the wonderful books filled with pictures and stories.

"How are you doing with your lessons?" Grandmamma asked.

"Not very well," said Heidi. "I don't think I will ever learn to read. My friend Peter was right—it is too hard."

"You haven't learned to read because you believed Peter," replied Grandmamma, "but I know that you can do it. When you are ready to try, it won't take long."

After being there a few weeks, Grandmamma realized that Heidi was unhappy about something. Heidi wouldn't tell her what it was. The truth was that Heidi was homesick and wanted to go back to her grandfather. She was afraid to say this because she thought Grandmamma and Clara wouldn't like her anymore if they knew she wanted to leave. This made Heidi feel trapped. She cried herself to sleep every night.

One day, Grandmamma asked the sad little girl, "Do you say your prayers at night?"

"No," said Heidi.

"Think how good it would be to tell everything to God. You can ask Him for the help you need."

"May I tell Him everything?" Heidi asked with a hopeful look.

"Yes, everything," Grandmamma answered.

Heidi ran to her room. She sat on her stool

and folded her hands. She asked God to help her go home.

About a week later, the tutor had good news for Mrs. Sesemann. Heidi was reading! Mrs. Sesemann went downstairs to see for herself. There was Heidi, reading out loud to Clara. That same night at supper, Heidi found a book with beautiful pictures lying on her plate. "It's yours now," Grandmamma told her.

"To keep? Even when I go home?" asked Heidi.

"Yes, forever," Grandmamma promised.

"But you're not going home for a long time, Heidi," said Clara. "When Grandmamma leaves, I want you to stay with me."

That night Heidi took the book to bed with her. The story she liked best was about a young shepherd. In the first picture, he was happily taking care of his father's flock. In the second picture, he had left home. This time he was thin and pale from not getting enough to eat. In the third picture, the boy went home and his father greeted him with open arms.

CHAPTER TEN

A Ghost in the House

Strange things were happening at the Sesemann house. Every morning, the servants came downstairs to find the front door open. They thought it must be a thief, but nothing was ever stolen. Could it be a ghost?

One night Sebastian and one of the other servants, John, stayed up to watch the front door. At midnight, they felt a cold wind and saw the door open.

"There was someone in white standing at the top of the stairs!" John told Miss Rottenmeier. "Then it *disappeared*!"

The next morning the housekeeper wrote to

Mr. Sesemann and asked him to come home. He did not believe there was really a ghost, but he decided to return, anyway. He was afraid that Clara would get sick if she were scared about a ghost in the house.

When he came home, Clara promised him that she was fine. She was even glad there was a ghost because it brought him home again so soon!

"How is the ghost?" he asked Miss Rottenmeier with a smile.

"It is no joke," replied the housekeeper. "Tomorrow morning you will believe me!"

"We'll see," he told her. Then he called for Sebastian. "Take a message to my friend the doctor. Ask him to come here tonight at nine o'clock. He will need to spend the night."

The doctor came over at nine o'clock just as Mr. Sesemann had asked. The girls and Miss Rottenmeier had already gone to bed. The doctor was a gray-haired man with friendly eyes. He laughed when he saw Mr. Sesemann. "You don't look sick at all! Why did you call me here to sit up all night with you?"

"There's a very good reason," said Mr. Sesemann. "My house is haunted!"

The doctor laughed. "Tell me about this ghost then."

The two men settled into the chairs in the study. Mr. Sesemann told the doctor how the front door was opened every night. Then they talked about other things. Soon after one o'clock, they heard the door open. The men picked up candles and went out into the hall. A small white figure stood in the doorway.

"It's Heidi! She's Clara's little friend," Mr. Sesemann told the doctor.

The doctor gently took the child by the hand. "Don't be scared. It's all right."

He took her upstairs and helped her into bed. "Where were you going?" he asked.

"I don't know," said Heidi.

"You were dreaming, weren't you?" the kind doctor asked.

"Yes. Every night I dream I am back with my grandfather, but when I wake up, I am still in Frankfurt."

"Are you happy here?" he asked.

Heidi started to cry. "I want to go back home to the mountain. It is so beautiful there! I just want to go home to Grandfather!"

"There, there, it's okay to cry," the doctor whispered. "Go to sleep now. Things will be better in the morning."

Then he went downstairs to Mr. Sesemann.

"Well, the little girl is a sleepwalker," the doctor told him. "She is your ghost! She is so homesick that she's not eating or sleeping. The poor child looks like a skeleton. You must send her back home right away."

CHAPTER ELEVEN

A Summer Evening on the Mountain

Early the next morning, Mr. Sesemann put everyone to work getting things ready for Heidi's trip back home.

Next Mr. Sesemann went to tell Clara what had happened. Clara was sad to lose her friend, but Mr. Sesemann promised that they could visit Heidi the next summer. Clara asked for Heidi's trunk to be brought to her room so she could add some special presents.

Mr. Sesemann told Sebastian to take Heidi back home on the train. They would go as far as Basel, Switzerland, that night. "And tonight at the hotel," he added, "make sure that the windows and doors are locked in her room. She walks in her sleep and we must keep her safe."

"Oh, *she* was the ghost!" exclaimed Sebastian.

Mr. Sesemann wrote a letter for Heidi's grandfather, explaining what had happened. When he finished, he called for Heidi. "You're going home today!" he told her.

"Home," whispered Heidi. She could barely breathe as she put on a new dress and hat.

When she went to say good-bye to Clara, there was a huge trunk in the middle of the girl's room.

"Come in," called Clara. "Do you like what I have packed for you?"

There were dresses, aprons, sewing things, and more. There was even a basket of soft white rolls for Peter's grandmother.

After she said good-bye to Clara, Heidi ran to her room to fetch her special book. She put it in the basket with the rolls. Then she opened her cupboard to find her old red shawl. She wrapped the shawl around something else and put it in the basket.

Mr. Sesemann was waiting by the carriage to say good-bye. Heidi thanked him for his kindness and added, "Please thank the doctor for me."

Heidi and Sebastian rode to Basel that night on the train, and then to Mayenfeld the next day. At the train station there, Sebastian found a man to drive Heidi and her trunk to Dörfli. The man was the miller in Dörfli and was taking sacks of flour home in his wagon. He told Sebastian that he would find someone to walk up the mountain with Heidi after they got to Dörfli.

"I can go by myself. I know the way very well," Heidi said with excitement.

Heidi's trunk was placed in the back and Sebastian lifted the young girl up onto the seat of the wagon. He gave Heidi a package that he said was a very important present from Mr. Sesemann. Then he handed her a letter for her grandfather. Heidi put them both in her basket. They shook hands and said good-bye.

The miller sat down beside Heidi in the wagon and headed toward the mountains. The miller had never met Heidi, but since Dörfli was such a small place, he knew all about her. "Didn't they treat you well in Frankfurt?" he asked.

"Oh, everyone there was very nice," Heidi told him. "But I would rather be on the mountain with Grandfather than anywhere else on earth!"

The miller began whistling and asked no more questions. Heidi was getting more excited with every minute. The town clock struck five when they drove into Dörfli.

As the miller helped Heidi down, she said quickly, "Thank you! Grandfather will come to get my trunk later."

Then she ran through the little town without stopping to talk to anyone. She climbed the mountain path as fast as she could with such a heavy basket. As soon as she saw Grandmother's

little house, Heidi started to run. She was out of breath when she went inside.

"It's me, Grandmother," cried Heidi. She dropped down on her knees at the woman's side.

Grandmother touched Heidi's curly hair and said, "God has answered my prayers!"

"Don't cry. I'll never go away again," Heidi promised. "Look what I brought for you."

She took the rolls out and piled them in Grandmother's lap.

"What a blessing!" the old woman exclaimed, touching the soft bread. "But you are the *greatest* blessing."

"Why, it's Heidi!" Peter's mother cried when she came in. "What a pretty dress you have on, and a hat with a feather, too."

"You can have the hat," replied Heidi. "I like mine better." She opened the red bundle and took out her funny-looking little hat. Brigitta told her to keep the hat with the feather, but Heidi hid it behind Grandmother's chair. She knew Brigitta would find it later. Then Heidi took off her dress and left on her petticoat.

"Why did you take off that pretty dress?" asked Brigitta.

"I want Grandfather to know it's me!"

Heidi said goodnight and started up the mountain with her basket on her arm. Heidi kept stopping to look all around at the beauty of the mountains.

Suddenly a warm glow fell on the grass at her feet. The snowfield turned red in the sunset and the rocks were glowing. The Alm Mountain was more beautiful than in all her dreams. Heidi stood looking at all this wonder and tears ran down her cheeks. She lifted her eyes to Heaven and thanked God for bringing her home.

Then she ran and ran until she came to Grandfather's hut. He was sitting on the bench, just like in the old days. Heidi threw down her basket, and rushed toward him. "Grandfather! Grandfather! Grandfather!" she cried over and over again.

Grandfather fell to his knees and hugged her. For the first time in years, there were tears in her grandfather's eyes.

"So you have come back, Heidi," he said. "Did they send you away?"

"Oh, no," said Heidi. "They were very nice, but all I wanted was to come home again.

Suddenly one morning Mr. Sesemann said to me... well, I think it was really the doctor's doing... but maybe it's all in the letter..." She went to get the package and the letter out of her basket.

The old man opened the package and saw that it held some money. "This belongs to you," Grandfather said, handing it to Heidi. Then he read the letter and put it in his pocket.

"Bring your money inside," he told her. "You can buy a bed and enough clothes for many years with it."

"I already have a bed," said Heidi, "and Clara sent so many dresses that I will never need any more."

"Put the money in the cupboard then. Some day you will want it."

Heidi skipped happily into the house. She was glad to see that nothing had changed. Then she went up to the hayloft.

"Grandfather," she called down, "my bed of hay is gone!"

"We can make it up again," he answered. "I did not know that you were coming back."

They heard a loud whistle. Heidi ran outside like a flash of lightning to see Peter and the goats.

Heidi called, "Good evening, Peter!" and then ran into the middle of the flock. "Little Swan! Little Bear! Do you remember me?"

The animals began rubbing their heads against her and *baa-aa*-ing loudly. Heidi hugged pretty little Snowflake and petted Greenfinch.

"I am glad you are back," said Peter, smiling widely. "Now we'll go together every day with the goats to the mountains again!"

When Heidi went inside, she found that Grandfather had made her a new bed out of fresh hay.

Grandfather got up several times that night to check on her, but Heidi was always sleeping soundly. She did not walk in her sleep because she was home at last.

CHAPTER TWELVE

Sunday Bells

The next day, Heidi went to visit Grandmother while her grandfather went to Dörfli to fetch her trunk. Grandmother told Heidi how much she liked eating the white rolls. Brigitta said that she knew her mother would get stronger if she could keep eating like that, but white rolls cost too much for her to buy.

Heidi had a great idea. "Oh, I have lots of money. I can buy you a fresh white roll every day, and two on Sunday. Peter can bring them up from Dörfli."

"No, child," answered Grandmother. "I can't let you do that."

Heidi would not change her mind. She thought of another nice surprise.

"I can read now, Grandmother! Would you like me to read from your prayer book?" Heidi asked.

"Oh, yes, my dear child."

Heidi climbed onto a chair and brought down the book. It had been sitting on the shelf a long time and was covered with dust. She cleaned it off and sat down. She turned a few pages and then began reading:

"Joy will be ours
In the garden blessed,
Where after the storm
We find our rest.
I wait in peace—
God's time is best."

The grandmother smiled. "Heidi, what comfort you bring me!"

Someone knocked on the window. Heidi looked out and saw her grandfather, who had come to walk her home. Brigitta tried to give Heidi the dress and hat she had left there the day before. Heidi took the dress, but not the hat, for she remembered how Grandfather had disliked Detie's "feathered hat."

On the way home, Heidi told her grandfather that she wanted to use her money to buy white rolls to help Grandmother grow stronger.

"The money is yours," he said. "You can buy bread for Grandmother for years to come."

Heidi shouted for joy. "Oh, Grandfather, everything is better now than it ever was before. We must thank God every day and never forget Him."

"What if someone *does* forget Him?" asked her grandfather in a quiet voice.

"If you run away from God, you will be sad and alone," Heidi told him, "but you can always go back to Him. Clara's Grandmamma told me so, and it was in the beautiful story in my book. I will read it to you when we get home."

Back at the hut, Grandfather sat down on the bench to think. Heidi went inside and brought out her book. She read him the story about the son who was happy at home, but who had left so that he could be his own master. The young man wasted the money that his father had given him.

He had to find work taking care of another man's pigs. There he had little to eat and only rags to wear. The young man kept thinking about how much he missed his father. He decided to go home and tell his father that he was sorry for everything.

"He was afraid his father would be angry," Heidi continued, "but the old man was filled with joy and welcomed him home. Isn't that beautiful, Grandfather?"

"Yes, it is," Grandfather answered. He looked very thoughtful.

That night, Grandfather got down on his knees and prayed, "Father, I have sinned and do not deserve to be called your son." Tears rolled down his cheeks.

Early the next morning he called, "Come along, Heidi! We're going to church!"

Heidi quickly put on her pretty dress from Frankfurt. "Why, Grandfather!" she exclaimed when she saw him. "You do look nice in your Sunday coat!"

The singing had already started when Heidi and her grandfather sat down in the back of the church. Everyone started whispering, "Look, Uncle is in church!"

After the sermon, Uncle and Heidi walked over to the pastor's house. The pastor greeted them warmly. Uncle had come to say he was sorry. "Pastor, you were right and I was wrong. I will find a home in Dörfli for the winter so Heidi can go to school."

"I am pleased to hear it," the pastor said.

They went outside and he shook Uncle's hand as if they were the best of friends. Everyone from church came over to shake Uncle's hand and welcome him back.

The old man's face shone with a new light.

"I am happier today than I deserve," he told Heidi. "God was good to me when He sent you to me."

CHAPTER THIRTEEN

A Surprise Visit from the Doctor

The kind doctor who had helped Heidi in Frankfurt was walking along the street near Clara's house. The day was bright and sunny, but he did not notice this. He kept his eyes on the ground and his face was very sad. His daughter had died and now he was alone, for his wife had died many years before.

"I'm glad you're here," said Mr. Sesemann when the doctor arrived. "Clara is feeling much better. We have already sent a telegram to Heidi to say that we will be visiting in a few days. Do you think Clara can go see Heidi?"

"Clara has been very sick. The trip would be

too much for her," said the doctor firmly. "She can go in the spring when she is stronger."

Mr. Sesemann knew Clara would be upset to hear this, but then he had an idea. "Doctor, I think *you* should take the trip and visit Heidi for us. It would be good for you to get away for a while."

Mr. Sesemann would not let his friend argue. He took him by the arm and led him to Clara's room. Tears filled Clara's eyes when she heard that she could not go, but she knew that they wanted what was best for her. She liked her father's plan to send the doctor.

"You will go see Heidi, won't you? You can come back and tell me all about it. I promise to take my medicine every day if you say yes."

The doctor smiled. "Then I will leave right away, Clara."

A few days later on the mountain, Peter asked Heidi if she would go with him and the goats.

"No, I am waiting for my friends to come," she answered.

"That's what you say every day now," Peter grumbled. He went off with the goats, swinging his stick.

Heidi went back inside to clean up, but it was just too nice a day to stay indoors. She kept running out to look down the path.

All of a sudden she saw them. "Grandfather, they are coming! Look, the doctor is in front of them!"

She ran to meet her old friend. "Good morning, Doctor. Thank you so much! Thank you for sending me home!"

The doctor had not expected such a nice welcome. He hoped that Heidi would not be sad when she heard his news.

"I am very sorry," he told her, "but Clara did not come. She has been sick and was not ready for a long trip. They will try to come in the spring."

Heidi was disappointed, but she knew that spring would come soon.

"They may even be able to stay longer in the spring," she told the doctor. "Come meet Grandfather."

Heidi had often talked about the kind doctor, so Grandfather greeted him as if he were an old friend. The doctor told them he would stay at the inn in Dörfli and come up the mountain every day to see them.

Since it was almost noon, Grandfather brought out the table from inside and set it up in front of the hut. Heidi ran to get the dishes for their lunch.

"Our food is plain, but the dining room is beautiful, isn't it?" Grandfather asked the doctor. He served them fresh milk, meat, and toasted cheese.

The doctor said the meal was the best he had eaten in a long time. "Clara must come up here. She would grow healthy and strong here."

As he spoke, a man came up the path. He was delivering a large package.

"That's the surprise Clara sent with me," said the doctor. He took off the outside wrapping. "There," he told Heidi. "Now you can do the rest."

Heidi happily opened the presents one by one. Clara had sent a thick shawl for Grandmother, plus rolls and cakes for her to eat. There was a warm winter coat for Heidi and many other small surprises. Clara had even put in a large sausage for Peter and his mother.

Later that afternoon, the three walked down the mountain. When they came to Peter's hut, Heidi said good-bye to the men. Grandfather said he would walk the doctor down to Dörfli and then come back for Heidi.

Heidi set the food next to Grandmother. She put the shawl across the old woman's knees and said, "This is from Clara and Grandmamma."

Grandmother touched the thick shawl. "What kind people they are! I never thought I would have anything as nice as this."

The next morning, the doctor walked up from Dörfli with Peter and the goats. He tried to talk with Peter, but the boy wouldn't answer, for he was not happy about sharing Heidi with anyone. Heidi was waiting when they came to Uncle's hut.

"Are you coming today?" Peter asked.

"Yes, if the doctor will come, too," replied Heidi. She couldn't think of a nicer treat for the doctor than going with the goats.

Grandfather brought out their lunch bag. He had put in extra meat and cheese so the doctor could have lunch with the children. Peter grinned when he felt how heavy the bag was.

As they walked, Heidi told the doctor all about the goats and their personalities. Peter felt left out and gave them grumpy looks.

Heidi showed the doctor her favorite spot and they sat down. There were flowers everywhere and the snow field sparkled in the sun. Heidi looked at the doctor to see if he liked it.

"Yes, Heidi," he told her. "I see how lovely everything is, but my heart is still sad."

"Have you told God why you are sad?"

"Yes," said the doctor. "But it doesn't help. God has sent me this trouble."

"Then you must remember that God has a plan for you. You just don't know what it is yet. I know something that might help you. It is from Grandmother's prayer book and I know it by heart:

"*Let not your heart be troubled if for a while it seems His mercy is gone. To those who wait in patience, He gives their heart's desire.*"

The doctor was sitting very still. His mother had read him the same prayer when he was a little boy.

"Heidi," he said, taking her hand, "that did make me feel better. Thank you."

By this time, Peter was a little angry. He had waited *so* long for Heidi to come with him, and now she was spending all her time with the doctor. When he saw that the sun was high in the sky, he grumpily called them to lunch.

The doctor said he wasn't hungry. All he wanted was some milk, so Heidi said she would just have milk, too. Peter started to feel better when he realized this meant he could eat all of the good things Uncle had sent for lunch.

The fall weather stayed bright and sunny. Each morning the doctor came to the hut. Some days he went with Heidi and Peter, other days he went exploring on the mountain with Uncle.

When it was time for the doctor to go home, Heidi walked part of the way to Dörfli with him.

As they said good-bye, the doctor said, "I wish I could take you to Frankfurt with me!"

"I would rather that you came back to us!" Heidi told him.

"You're right. I'll do that. Good-bye, Heidi." Heidi could see tears in his eyes. He turned away quickly.

Heidi started to cry, too. "I will come to Frankfurt with you if you need me, but first I must run back and tell Grandfather."

"No," he said gently. "You must stay here where you are happy. I *will* ask you this favor—if I am ever sick and alone, will you come stay with me then?"

"Yes, I love you nearly as much as Grandfather," replied Heidi.

She waved until he was out of sight.

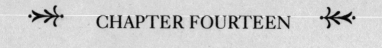

CHAPTER FOURTEEN

Winter in Dörfli

As soon as the first snow fell, Heidi and Grandfather moved down to Dörfli. Grandfather rented an old house near the church and started fixing it up.

After a few days in their new home, Heidi wanted to go see Grandmother, but her grandfather said, "No, not today, or even tomorrow. The snow is too deep now, Heidi. Wait until it freezes on top."

Heidi went to school in Dörfli every day and loved to learn new things. She didn't see Peter much because he didn't like to go to school, but sometimes he visited Heidi in the evenings.

After many days, the top of the snow was finally frozen hard. Peter was happy to see this because it meant that Heidi could come for a visit. He ate his breakfast in a hurry and said, "I must be off to school."

Peter got onto his sled and shot down the mountain. He went like lightning! When he reached Dörfli, he decided to keep on going. (He was *sure* that he could not stop the sled when it was going *so* fast.)

When he finally *did* stop, he was all the way past Dörfli—and Mayenfeld, too! He knew it was already too late to go to school, so he decided to take his time and walk back. By the time he got to Uncle's house it was noon. Heidi was home from school, eating lunch with her grandfather.

"The snow is frozen hard," he told Heidi and Grandfather.

"I can go see Grandmother!" said Heidi happily. "But why didn't you come to school today?"

"The sled carried me too far," he answered.

"What would you do if your goats ran away and did not do what was good for them?" asked Uncle.

"I would beat them," replied Peter.

"Then remember this—next time you miss school, come to me and get what you deserve."

Peter looked around to see if Uncle had a stick like the one he used on his goats! But Uncle said in a cheerful voice, "Come eat with us. Then you can take Heidi to see your grandmother."

At Peter's house, Heidi was surprised to find Grandmother in bed. She wasn't sick, but she said that the cold had gotten into her bones.

"Grandmother, your bed is not right," Heidi noticed. "Your head is too low."

"I know, child," said Grandmother. "The pillow is old and flat."

"I wish I had brought my Frankfurt bed home with me," said Heidi. "There were three big pillows on it. I bet they would help you sleep better."

"Let's not talk about that," Grandmother replied. "I am lucky to have so many nice things already, like this shawl and the nice bread you get for me. Best of all is seeing you, Heidi. Will you read to me today?"

Heidi got down the old book and read aloud to Grandmother. She ended with one of her favorite poems.

My heart is sad, my eyes grow dim,
Yet still I put my trust in Him.
For someday when all sorrow's past,
To heavenly arms I'll come at last.

"Thank you, Heidi," said Grandmother. "When you read to me, my heart is happy."

Then Heidi kissed Grandmother good-bye.

It was already dark, but the moon was shining brightly on the snow. The children flew down the mountain on Peter's sled like birds through the air.

The next day, Peter was at school right on time. After he was done, he went to see Heidi.

"I have the best idea, Peter!" Heidi told him. She was very excited. "I'm going to teach you to read so you can read to your grandmother every day."

"I don't want to," he grumbled.

Heidi was angry to hear this. "If you don't try to learn, I will tell your mother to send you to the boys' school in Frankfurt. The teachers are mean. They wear black clothes and tall hats. You would not like it there!"

A shiver ran down Peter's back. "All right, I'll try."

Heidi brought out an ABC book that Clara had sent her. She sat at the table by Peter and opened it. Peter tried to read the first sentence, but couldn't get it right.

"I will read it to you once, then it will be easier for you," Heidi decided. She read:

"A B C must be learned today,
Or else the judge will make you pay."

"I won't do it," said Peter stubbornly.

"Won't do what?"

"I won't pay the judge!"

"Well, learn those three letters and you won't have to," Heidi told him.

❄ ❄ ❄

As the winter went by, Peter slowly learned all of his letters, and then Heidi helped him learn to read sentences.

One evening, Peter walked into his house and said, "I can do it now." He took down the book of prayers and began to read.

"Who would have thought it possible?" said his proud mother.

There was a reading lesson the next day at school. The teacher asked, "Do you want us to skip you again today, Peter? Or will you try one more time?"

Peter read three sentences without any mistakes.

The teacher stared at him. "I have been trying to teach you your letters for years, and now suddenly you can read! How did this happen?"

"It was Heidi," answered Peter.

"I won't do it," said Peter stubbornly.

"Won't do what?"

"I won't pay the judge!"

"Well, learn those three letters and you won't have to," Heidi told him.

❄ ❄ ❄

As the winter went by, Peter slowly learned all of his letters, and then Heidi helped him learn to read sentences.

One evening, Peter walked into his house and said, "I can do it now." He took down the book of prayers and began to read.

"Who would have thought it possible?" said his proud mother.

There was a reading lesson the next day at school. The teacher asked, "Do you want us to skip you again today, Peter? Or will you try one more time?"

Peter read three sentences without any mistakes.

The teacher stared at him. "I have been trying to teach you your letters for years, and now suddenly you can read! How did this happen?"

"It was Heidi," answered Peter.

The teacher said, "I have noticed another change, Peter. You used to skip school, but now you come every day. Who brought this about?"

"It was Uncle," Peter told him.

CHAPTER FIFTEEN

A Joyful Visit in the Spring

At last, spring came. The grass turned green again and even the wind sounded happy. Heidi and Grandfather were back home on the mountain.

One morning when Peter brought up the goats, he had a letter for Heidi.

She danced with joy when she read it. "It's from Clara! They're coming soon!" She ran into the shed where Grandfather was working so she could read it to him. Peter followed her to listen.

Dear Heidi,

We're leaving in just a few days! The doctor tells us every day how much he enjoyed his visit with you. "No one can help but to get well up there," he tells me. I can't wait to see everything for myself!

We will stop in Ragatz for six weeks, then come on to Dörfli. Father has to go to Paris, France, on business. But Grandmamma is coming with me and can't wait to see you.

Your friend, Clara

Peter rushed out at the end. He was angry to think he would lose Heidi again to visitors from Frankfurt.

The visitors finally came on a beautiful morning at the end of June. Heidi and Grandfather watched as a strange parade climbed the mountain path. In front, two men carried Clara in a fancy chair. Next came Grandmamma, riding a white horse. At the back, there was a man pushing Clara's empty wheelchair and another man carrying a large bundle.

The men set Clara's chair down near the hut. The girls hugged each other happily. Grandmamma climbed down and said hello to Heidi and her grandfather.

"What a beautiful place, Uncle!" exclaimed Grandmamma. "My Heidi looks so well—like a wild rose!"

"Oh, Grandmamma, I could stay here forever," Clara said. "I've never seen such a beautiful place."

"I think you will feel better in your usual chair, little daughter," Grandfather told Clara. He lifted her gently and moved her into the wheelchair.

Grandfather then brought out the table and extra chairs so they could eat lunch outside. "I never enjoyed anything as much as this," Grandmamma said as they ate. "Did I really see you taking a second piece of toasted cheese, Clara?"

"It tastes better than all the fancy food we had in Ragatz," said Clara.

"The mountain air makes it taste so good," answered Uncle.

Before they went down to Dörfli for the night, Grandmamma and Clara wanted to see inside the hut. Clara's wheelchair was too big to go through the door, so Uncle carried her inside.

Grandmamma was pleased to see how neat everything was. She even went up the ladder to see Heidi's bed in the hayloft.

"What a nice place to sleep!" Heidi followed her and Uncle carried Clara up.

"You can see the sky right from your bed!" Clara exclaimed when she saw the little round window.

Uncle looked at Grandmamma. "I have been thinking," he said. "If you agree, your granddaughter could stay with us. She would grow stronger here. I would be happy to look after her."

Grandmamma smiled. "I was thinking the same thing! Thank you, Uncle."

Grandmamma helped make a bed in the hayloft for Clara. She ran her hand carefully over the mattress to make sure no hay was sticking up. When she went back down, Uncle said he thought Clara should stay for a month. Grandmamma said yes and the girls clapped their hands.

The girls went outside to say good-bye to Grandmamma. She decided that since Clara was staying with Heidi, she would go back to Ragatz. After Grandmamma mounted her horse, Uncle took the bridle and led her down the mountain path to Dörfli.

While Grandfather was gone, Peter came down with the goats. Clara was happy to finally meet little Snowflake, lively Greenfinch, and the others, but Peter would not come over to talk with her.

That night as Clara and Heidi lay on their beds in the hayloft, Clara looked out the open window. "Heidi, it is beautiful up here—it is like looking into Heaven."

"Do you know why the stars are so happy?" asked Heidi.

"No, why?" Clara asked her.

"Because they live in Heaven and know how well God takes care of us."

The two children said their prayers, and then Heidi put her head down on her arm and went right to sleep. Clara lay awake for a long time, looking out in wonder at the stars.

Clara was just waking up the next morning when Grandfather came up to get her. She had slept well and was excited about the new day.

When Heidi woke up, she was surprised to see Clara already dressed. She hurried to get ready, too. During the night, Grandfather had widened the doorway so that Clara's chair could

go in and out. He wheeled her out into the sunshine. Heidi sat with her friend while Grandfather went to take care of the goats.

The morning wind blew gently on the girls' faces and they could smell the fir trees.

Grandfather brought them each a bowl of milk. Clara wasn't sure she would like goat's milk, but she gave it a try. She thought it tasted like sugar and cinnamon, and drank every drop.

Peter then came with the goats. "Come with me!" he called to Heidi.

"I can't while Clara is here," Heidi told him, "but Grandfather will bring us up the mountain another day."

Peter was not happy to hear this.

Clara and Heidi spent the day talking about all the things that had happened since they were together in Frankfurt.

Later, when Peter came back with the goats, he still looked grumpy. He would not talk to the girls when they called out to him.

Clara watched Grandfather take Little Swan and Little Bear into their shed. She was suddenly hungry.

"Isn't it funny?" she said, surprised at herself. "For a long time, I only ate because I had to. But now here I am, excited that Grandfather is bringing us milk."

That night, Clara fell asleep as soon as she lay down on her bed. She slept soundly all night, which she usually did not do at home.

After a few weeks, Grandfather asked Clara to try something new. "Won't you try to stand for a minute or two, little daughter?"

Clara tried, but said that it hurt to put her feet down. Each day, though, she tried to stand a little longer.

CHAPTER SIXTEEN

One Little Push

One morning, Grandfather pushed Clara's wheelchair outside and then went back in to wake up the girls.

While he was inside, Peter came by with the goats. Looking around to make sure no one was watching, he gave the chair a big push. The chair rolled faster and faster down the slope. Peter hid behind a bush, but peeked out to see what would happen. The chair bounced several times and then pieces of it flew in every direction. Now Heidi's friend would have to go home! Peter ran up the path.

When Heidi came out with Grandfather and Clara, the wheelchair was gone. The wind was blowing hard, and the shed door was banging against the wall.

"The chair is gone! Do you think the wind blew it down the hill, Grandfather?" Heidi cried. "Now we can't go up the mountain!"

"We can still go up the mountain," Grandfather said. "I will come back and look for the chair. I wonder why Peter isn't here yet? Well, let's go on without him." Heidi walked with their goats and Grandfather carried Clara.

Farther up the mountain, they were surprised to find Peter lying on the ground.

"Why didn't you stop for my goats, you lazy rascal?" Grandfather wanted to know.

Peter sat up fast. "No one was up," he lied.

"Have you seen the chair?" Grandfather asked.

"What chair?" replied Peter.

Grandfather said no more. Heidi spread a shawl out in a sunny spot and Grandfather settled Clara on it. He told the girls they could stay and eat lunch with Peter. He would come back for them in the afternoon.

As the day passed, Heidi grew tired of staying in one place. She wanted to look at the flowers, but didn't want to leave Clara alone. Then she had an idea. She picked a bunch of green leaves and brought Snowflake over to Clara to keep her company. The little goat lay down and Clara fed her the leaves. Clara felt a strange new happiness as she sat here alone with the goat. Suddenly she wished that she could get well and do everything for herself.

Heidi came running back. "The flowers are so beautiful. You must come see them! I know— I'll carry you!"

Clara shook her head. "No, you are too small to carry me."

Heidi looked at Peter. He was sitting a short distance away, just staring at them. She called, "Peter, come down here!"

He didn't get up, so she shouted, "Peter, if you don't come right now, you'll be sorry!"

Heidi meant that she would not share her lunch with Peter, but Peter did not know this. He was feeling guilty and was afraid she knew what he had done to Clara's chair, so he hurried over.

"Put one arm around my neck, Clara," Heidi

said, "and put the other through Peter's arm. Then lean on us and we'll be able to carry you."

Peter was tall and Heidi was short, so poor Clara went up and down with every step. Clara cried out a little at first, but with each step, it hurt less to put her feet down and she felt safer. Heidi was so happy to see this!

"You can walk, Clara! Now we can come up here every day and go where we like. Isn't this wonderful?"

Clara agreed. She could think of no greater joy than to walk like other people.

Soon they reached the flowers that Heidi wanted to show Clara. Peter fell asleep, but Heidi ran about. Clara sat quietly and thought about how happy she felt.

At noon, Heidi went to get the lunch bag. She gave each of them an equal share of the food. Peter ended up with twice as much because the girls gave him what they couldn't eat. He felt too guilty to enjoy it.

When her grandfather came back, Heidi couldn't wait to tell him what happened. He hurried over to Clara and said with a big smile, "So you've done it!"

He helped her walk a little way and it was even easier than before. She soon grew tired, so he picked her up and told her it was time to go home and rest.

That evening in Dörfli, Peter came upon a group of people staring at something on the ground. He pushed his way through and found what was left of Clara's chair.

"It must have been worth a fortune," said the baker. "How did this happen?"

"Uncle said the wind might have done it," one of the women said.

"It's a good thing that it was the wind and not a person," said the baker, "or he would have to pay for it."

Peter ran home as fast as he could.

The next morning, Grandfather suggested that they invite Grandmamma for a visit to show her that Clara could walk. The girls wanted to surprise her so they invited Grandmamma to visit in about a week. That would give Clara time to practice her walking.

The following days were exciting for Clara. She awoke each morning with a happy voice. "I am well now! I am well now!" she sang out.

"I won't have to use my chair! I will walk like other people!"

Every day, with Grandfather's help, she found it easier and easier to take steps. And every day she grew stronger and hungrier! The good milk and delicious bread and cheese improved her health and made her cheeks rosy. And the mountain air filled her with hope and joy.

CHAPTER SEVENTEEN

The Best Surprise of All

Grandmamma sent them a letter the day before she left so that the children would be waiting for her. Peter brought Uncle the letter and then ran off quickly. Heidi thought Peter looked like he was afraid of something.

In the morning, Grandfather picked a large bunch of flowers to welcome Clara's grandmother and Heidi cleaned the hut. When the girls were dressed, they went outside to wait. At last, they saw Grandmamma on a horse coming up the path.

Grandmamma climbed down from her horse, and was shocked to see Clara sitting on the bench and not in her wheelchair. "Is it really you, dear child? Your cheeks are so round and rosy now! And why aren't you in your chair?" she asked.

Then came the big surprise!

Heidi helped Clara stand up. The two of them started walking toward Grandmamma, with Clara leaning on Heidi's shoulder. Laughing and crying, the lady ran to them and hugged them

both. Then she saw Uncle, watching with a smile on his face.

"My dear Uncle, how much we have to thank you for! It is your caring and nursing…"

"And God's sun and mountain air," he added.

"Don't forget the beautiful milk I've been drinking!" added Clara.

"You've grown stronger and taller, too!" said her grandmother. "I must send your father a telegram right away to give him the happy news. Uncle, how can I send a telegram?"

"Peter can take it for you." He whistled loudly.

Peter knew that whistle and came running. The boy was white as a ghost, afraid that he was going to be punished. Instead, Uncle gave him a note and told him to take it to the post office in Dörfli.

After Peter left, the girls told Grandmamma how Grandfather had helped Clara to stand a little bit every day. Then they explained how the beautiful flowers up on the mountains had helped to push Clara into taking her first walk.

Meanwhile, Mr. Sesemann had finished his business in Paris and was working on a surprise of his own. Without telling anyone, he had come to

Dörfli and was at that moment taking the long hike up the mountain.

There were so many paths, Mr. Sesemann was afraid he was on the wrong one. When he saw a boy running down the mountain, he called out, "Is this the way to the hut where the old man and Heidi live?"

The boy was Peter. He thought the man must be a policeman. Peter was so scared that he fell and went rolling down the mountain. Along the way he lost the telegram. Finally he stopped and caught his breath. He knew that Uncle would be angry if he left the goats alone too long, so he began climbing back up the path.

Luckily Mr. Sesemann was on the right path and ended up at Uncle's hut. As he came closer, two girls walked toward him. There was a little girl with curly hair and a tall one with pink cheeks. Mr. Sesemann stopped short when he realized the tall girl was Clara. His eyes filled with tears and he could not speak.

"Don't you know me, Papa?" called Clara, beaming with happiness. "Have I changed that much since you saw me last?"

He ran over and hugged her tightly.

"Yes, indeed you are changed!" he said with tears in his eyes. "Are you really my Clara? My dear little Clara. Oh, my dear little Clara."

"Well, what do you say?" Grandmamma exclaimed. "You thought you were surprising us, but it is nothing compared to our surprise for you!" She gave him a kiss. "Now come and meet Uncle who has made this happen."

CHAPTER EIGHTEEN

Good-bye 'Til We Meet Again

While Mr. Sesemann talked with Uncle, Grandmamma and the girls walked behind the hut to see the fir trees. Grandmamma found a bunch of beautiful flowers waiting there for her. She asked, "Heidi, did you pick these for me?"

"No," said Heidi, "but I know who did!"

At this moment, they heard a noise behind the trees. It was Peter. He was trying to sneak around behind the house so the men out front would not hear him. He was afraid the man with Uncle was a policeman.

"Come here, boy," Grandmamma said. "Did you do it?"

Peter was looking at the ground, so he didn't see that Grandmamma was pointing to the flowers. "Yes," he said quietly. "Now it is broken and no one can fix it."

Mr. Sesemann and Uncle came around the corner. Grandmamma asked Uncle, "What is wrong with this boy? He makes no sense."

"He is fine," Uncle promised. He had seen Peter's angry looks at Clara, so he figured out what happened. "He was the wind that pushed the wheelchair down the slope. Now he thinks he's going to be punished."

Grandmamma was surprised to hear this. Peter did not look like a bad boy to her. "No, we will not punish him any further. Here are all these strangers who come and keep his best friend away from him. His anger just got the upper hand."

She went over to Peter and sat down next to him. "I have something to tell you," she said softly. "Stop shaking and try to listen. It was wrong of you to push the chair down the mountain. You knew this, yes? You must remember that God is watching, even when no one else is. When you do something wrong,

He keeps pricking you until you fix things. Have you felt something like that, Peter?"

Peter nodded. That was exactly how he had been feeling.

"The trouble you caused turned out to be a good thing," added Grandmamma. "Clara had no chair, so she learned to walk. So now this matter is over. I do want you to have something happy that will remind you of the visitors from Frankfurt. What would you like?"

Peter couldn't believe that he was going to get a present after all this. He felt like the weight of a mountain had fallen off of him. He had to admit one more thing: "I lost the paper, too."

"You are a good boy to tell me," said Grandmamma. "Now what can I give you?"

He thought about the fancy knives and whistles he saw every summer at the fair. They all cost a penny and he never had that much. He couldn't decide which to ask for, so he finally just asked for a penny. He could decide later what to buy.

"That's easy," Grandmamma said, laughing. She pulled out her purse and put four silver coins in his hand, with some pennies on top. "Here are as many pennies as there are weeks in the year. Every Sunday you'll have a penny to spend."

Peter thought he must be dreaming to have all this money. He ran off to tell his mother.

After supper that night, Mr. Sesemann asked Uncle what he could do to thank him. "With the help of God, you have made my child well, when all my money could do nothing to help her. What can I do to show you my thanks?"

Uncle smiled. "Seeing your daughter well and happy is my reward," he replied. "I have all I need to take care of Heidi, but I have nothing to leave her when I die. She has no one but me— and Detie, who has taken so little care of her. If you could promise me that Heidi will never have to live with strangers, that is my only wish."

"She is part of our family now, too," promised Mr. Sesemann, shaking Uncle's hand.

He also told Uncle that their old friend, the doctor, was planning to move to Dörfli. "He has never felt as happy as when he was here with you both. Now there will be two of you to watch over Heidi!"

Grandmamma put her arm around Heidi. "Is there anything you wish for, child?"

Heidi knew just what she wanted. "I want the bed I slept in at Frankfurt. It is for Peter's grandmother, so she will be warm and able to breathe better."

"What a dear child you are," said Grandmamma. "I will telegraph Miss Rottenmeier at once and have her pack up the bed. It should be here in two days. Why don't we go meet Grandmother on our way back to Dörfli?"

Uncle took Clara in his arms and they all walked down to Peter's hut. Heidi ran to give the old woman a hug.

"Grandmother! We're getting you a new bed! It has thick pillows and a warm bedspread. Grandmamma's having it sent right away," said the excited girl.

The old woman smiled sadly. "She must be a kind lady. I should be glad that she is taking you with her."

"No, we are not taking Heidi away from you," said Grandmamma kindly. "She is going to stay here. We will come and visit her every year."

The old grandmother's face filled with joy. She pressed the other woman's hand. "God has sent me so many good things. He never forgets us, does He?"

"No, He doesn't," replied Grandmamma. "Now we must say good-bye, but only until next summer."

Many things happened in the weeks that followed. The bed arrived from Frankfurt and Grandmother is already getting stronger.

The doctor has moved to Dörfli. He bought the old house where Uncle and Heidi lived in the winter, and is fixing it up. He will share the house with Heidi and her grandfather when they are in town. There will be a warm stall out back for the goats to sleep in.

The doctor and Uncle become better friends every day. The doctor has promised that he will always look after Heidi. "She will be like a daughter to me," he said, "and I will treat her that way in my Will. She will have nothing to fear when we are both gone." Nothing could have pleased Uncle more.

Heidi and Peter are—at this moment—sitting with Grandmother. So many things have happened since last summer that they have much to talk about. It's hard to say which of them looks the happiest at being together again.

THE END

ABOUT THE AUTHOR

JOHANNA SPYRI

Johanna Heusser was born in 1827 in the town of Hirzel, Switzerland. Like her most famous character, Heidi, Johanna grew up surrounded by the beauty of the Alps. She was the fourth of six children. Her father was a doctor and her mother worked in a hospital. She lived in Hirzel until she was 25, when she married a young lawyer, Bernhard Spyri, and moved to the city of Zurich. They had one son.

Spyri did not begin her writing career until she was 43. She published her early work anonymously, including the first stories about Heidi. The full novel was published in 1881 to raise money for war charities.

Sadly, both her husband and son died before her. Spyri continued to write—in all more than 48 stories. But it was *Heidi* that brought her fame and a lasting place of honor in children's literature. For more than a century, the story of this irresistible orphan has captured the hearts of readers of all ages.

Spyri was a deeply religious person and she donated much of her earnings to charity. She died in Zurich in 1901.